## Owl Pals™

Owl Pals Publishing, Bellevue, WA 98004 USA

First Edition, October 2007

ISBN 978-0-9799196-8-8

Printed in China

Please visit us at owlpals.com

# THE OWLS
## of the
# ENCHANTED FOREST

By

KEITH HARARY

Illustrated by

LUBA GONINA

**Owl Pals**™
Owl Pals Publishing
Bellevue, WA

*F*or everyone who dreams of making the world a better place.

1

The Enchanted Forest was
a place on a high plateau at the
meeting point of two great rivers.
It was a magical place where the
water tumbled down in crystal falls
from the surrounding mountains
on its way to the ocean below.

In the daylight,
the sky was a pale blue-green.
At night, it glowed and sparkled with the
lights of an undiscovered city on the far horizon.

2

$\mathcal{I}$t was a place inhabited by mystical creatures
who were unlike any other beings that existed
in any other forest or any other world.

They were all very
different, but they were all owls.

4

Some of the owls had human features. They dressed in shirts and vests, and one even wore spats covering his talons.

Some had bare feet with wrinkled toes that made them look like a cross between a person and a bird.

Some were equipped with wheels instead of feet. Others had normal claws of different sizes.

There was one who rode a musical magic carpet.

There was another with turquoise eyes who had billowy plumage all around her head.

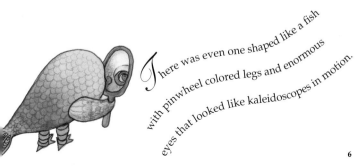

There was even one shaped like a fish with pinwheel colored legs and enormous eyes that looked like kaleidoscopes in motion.

Some of the owls were always serious.
Others were constantly amused.

Some always seemed to be surprised.
Others looked like nothing could surprise them.

*S*ome looked elegant and stylish
while others looked like brightly
colored clowns with wings.

*S*ome looked like the owls
who lived in any ordinary forest, except
that there was nothing commonplace about them.

$\mathcal{T}$he owls always knew that they were created by the Artist
who lived in the City on the Other Side of the Horizon.
In that time, on one particularly bright day, the Artist
sat in his studio and looked out his window
and across the rooftops toward the clouds
above the distant mountains. It was late
afternoon on the first day of Spring.

$\mathcal{T}$he air was filled with sounds of children playing
and the fragrance of flowers bursting into bloom.
The clouds appeared to form the shape of an
enormous owl floating on a gentle breeze across the sky.

11

The Artist sat at his easel
as he looked out the window and
thought about what he might paint.

The Artist always loved the city with all of its excitement. But he also wished that people would take more time to help each other and enjoy their surroundings.

$\mathcal{T}$he Artist tried to imagine what
it would be like to live in a place where
people had more time to listen, and where they
also took the time to make the world a better place.

14

$\mathcal{A}$s he thought about those things, the
Artist fell into a dream. In his dream, he became
the owl that he saw floating in the clouds above
the mountains. He felt connected not only to the
human world, but also to all of nature, including
every living creature. He felt especially connected
to the world of owls, because ~ in that particular
moment ~ he felt that he also was an owl,
even though he was having a dream.

$\mathcal{H}$e began to form his thoughts
into the shapes of other clouds surrounding
him, so that they looked like strange,
imaginary combinations of people
and birds that floated with
him in the air above
the mountains.

The Artist watched the little creatures being formed out of his thoughts and floating all around him in the sky. "I wish that I could be this creative," he thought, "whenever I'm painting pictures in my studio." He thought about coloring the fluffy white birds in all of their fantastic forms with splashes of paint that would bring them to life.

In that instant, one of the owls suddenly took on an unusual combination of colors, in pastel shades of blue and lavender mixed with the white of the clouds, and spoke to him.

"*Creativity,*" said the owl. "You have to believe that I fit that description." The owl was wearing a pale blue shirt with a gold pocket watch and chain clipped to the pocket on his elegant purple vest.

*H*is wings appeared to be a glorious cloak made of purple, blue and lavender feathers. There were also lavender feathers around the ankles of his bare, human feet. "I'll teach the world about being creative," he said. "Now think of another interesting possibility, and you can create another owl."

"*T*hat's a big responsibility," said the Artist.
In that moment, a pair of colorful owls emerged
out of the flock that formed within the clouds.
It was a parent owl with a tiny baby.

They were green and orange with ordinary
claws for feet, and dark blue eyes surrounded by a
mask that had a warm ginger glow like the moonlight.

"We'll be *Responsibility*," they said.
The Artist began to understand that all of his ideas
were not only bringing the owls to life ~

they were giving each of them a special focus.

"I hope I know what I'm doing," he thought. Another owl was splashed with colors. His eyes were explosions of black and white feathers, surrounded by circles of gold that made them look like a pair of sunflowers that were bursting wide open. All the rest of his feathers were the color of autumn leaves in various shades of orange, gold and green.

"I'll be *Hope*," said the owl.

*B*efore long, the Artist produced an entire flock of
colorful owls that appeared out of the clouds.

There was *Curiosity*

in all of her magnificent green
and turquoise plumage, looking
enthralled by all the fascinating things
that life would give her to discover.
She had powerful springs in her legs
that made it possible for her to
bound into the air whenever
something out of reach
attracted her attention.

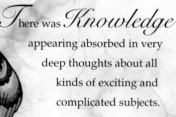

There was *Knowledge*

appearing absorbed in very
deep thoughts about all
kinds of exciting and
complicated subjects.

There was *Forgiveness*, *Joy*, *Enthusiasm* and *Ability*.

There was *Generosity* and *Communication*.

There were also dozens of other owls representing the best ideas that the Artist wanted to help bring out into the world.

The owls floated around
him in the sky, but had no place
to land. The Artist looked
down at the mountainside
and imagined a home for
the owls that was a unique
and protected place on
the edge of the rest of
the world. It was a
magnificent plateau
with waterfalls and
wild trees of every
possible variety.
It appeared where
there had only
been a small
outcropping
in the rocks
before.

"*I* give you independence," said the Artist,
and one last owl appeared out of the clouds.

"I will be *Independence*," said the owl.

29

$\mathcal{H}$e had shining gold feathers with watermelon and raspberry highlights. Instead of feet, he had an oblong wheel that he could use like a unicycle to move along the ground. He was the first owl to land in the Enchanted Forest that would become their secret sanctuary. The other owls followed him to their new home.

The Artist woke up back in his studio in the City on the Other Side of the Horizon. It was getting close to sunset. He saw the early moonlight coming through the window as the daytime sky began to change into the night. "That's the most incredible dream I've ever had," he thought. He looked at his easel and thought about the pictures he wanted to paint of all the remarkable owls that he imagined in his dream. He sat at the easel and started to paint.

$\mathcal{T}$he Artist painted a portrait of Enthusiasm, flying on
his magic carpet. Then he painted Ability riding on the wheels
he had in place of feet, the owl's pale gray eyes surrounded
by glowing red circles and carrot colored feathers as he
rolled across the forest underneath a harvest moon. The
Artist painted Forgiveness with her orange beak and pale blue
feathers, and butterfly wings that were woven of colorful silk.

$\mathscr{H}$e painted a dozen different owls through
the night, until the sun came up the following day and
he could hear the sounds of morning waking all around him.

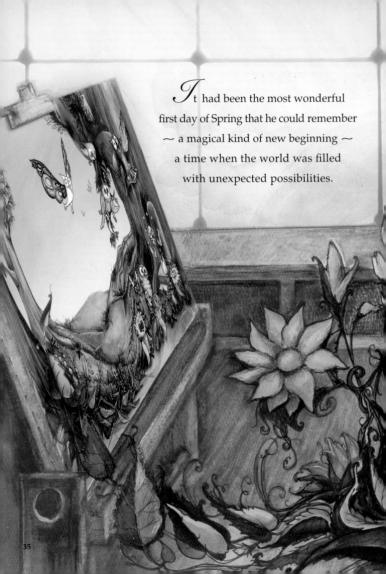

$\mathcal{I}$t had been the most wonderful
first day of Spring that he could remember
~ a magical kind of new beginning ~
a time when the world was filled
with unexpected possibilities.

$\mathcal{B}$ut perhaps the most unexpected possibility of all was something that even the Artist couldn't yet imagine ∼ that all of the owls he created in his dream had really come to life in the Enchanted Forest on the other side of the horizon. He never expected that they would be coming to find him, and that together they would change the world.